STATE OF MI

State of Mind

Martha Ronk

NEW AMERICAN POETRY SERIES: 21

SUN & MOON PRESS
LOS ANGELES · 1995

Sun & Moon Press
A Program of The Contemporary Arts Educational Project, Inc.
a nonprofit corporation
6026 Wilshire Boulevard, Los Angeles, California 90036

This edition first published in paperback in 1995 by Sun & Moon Press
10 9 8 7 6 5 4 3 2 1
FIRST EDITION
©1995 by Martha Ronk
Biographical material ©1995 by Sun & Moon Press
All rights reserved

Some of these poems previously appeared in *Chelsea Magazine, Crazy Horse, Denver Quarterly, Hambone, o-blēk,* and *Talisman.* The author wishes to thank the editors of these magazines.

This book was made possible, in part, through
an operational grant from the Andrew W. Mellon Foundation, and
through contributions to
The Contemporary Arts Educational Project, Inc.,
a nonprofit corporation

Cover: André Kertesz *à ma fenêtre*
Design: Katie Messborn
Typography: Guy Bennett

LIBRARY OF CONGRESS CATALOGING IN PUBLICATION DATA
Ronk, Martha Clare.
State of Mind / Martha Ronk.
p. cm — (New American Poetry Series: 21)
ISBN: 1-55713-236-4 (alk. paper)
I. Title. II. Series: New American Poetry Series; NAP 21
PS3568.O5745S73 1995
811'.54—dc20
95-43165
CIP

Printed in the United States of America on acid-free paper.

Without limiting the rights under copyright reserved here, no part of this publication may be reproduced, stored in or introduced into a retrieval system, or transmitted, in any form or by any means (electronic, mechanical, photocopying, recording or otherwise), without the prior written permission of both the copyright owner and the above publisher of the book.

Contents

STATE OF TRANSITION
   California   9
   A State of Transition   10
   Arroyo Seco   11
   The San Gabriels   12
   Not Knowing the Language   13
   Paraphrase   14
   Fire at Midnight   15
   The Blue Cold   16
   Griffith Park   17
   The Bus   18
   Driving   19
   Cactus   20
   The Counterfeiters   21
   Pico Boulevard   22
   Neutra's Window   23
   Drowning   24
   Sunset   25
   The Statues   26
   The Photograph   27
   Dream   28

First Street   29
The Sierras   30
The Hollywood Hills   31
No Man's Land   32
The Real   33
The Moon over LA   34

NOT JUST A PRONOUN   35

OTHER MINDS
"wings of the dove"   55
"divertimento"   56
"absence"   57
"the Dubliners"   58
"stranger than fiction"   59
"the store"   60
"the garden"   61
"end of summer"   62
"pride and prejudice"   63
"mythic birds"   64
"no tomorrow"   65
"night and day"   66
"happenstance"   67
"accidents will happen"   68
"the great blue"   69
"the golden bowl"   70
"the missing body"   71
"equivalents"   72

State of Transition

California

The question of other minds is the question.
Not only snow and oranges on a postcard
of Carmelita flowers found in a geographical distance
which also questions the possibility of disaster
or the hand of God before the land rumbles
or thunder crosses the plains.
What can't be is the assumption by which she feels her way.
Is she curious for sexual reasons
or because he ended his life?
Or why animosity sprang to her lips.
You could see through the cracks
you could hear Santa Anas coming up in dry boards.
Or to take half a step back where windows opened
on fronds spilling dust and other minds.

A State of Transition

At the threshold between recognition and not
in the blurred figure going in and out
before facial expressions or the lifelike sentence
at the core of being in a state of transition
for over twenty years. Edged off the map
and unable to hear what you are saying
in an effort to describe the blank confusion
of hybiscus and oleander spilling through the French doors
into lives myopically out of focus
stumbling forward all elbows all knees.

Arroyo Seco

The gap in logic cuts a dry riverbed across the land
unerring in inference and what follows from what isn't there
eroded about the edges of metaphor
where redwood and imported palm catch a glimpse
of the new world. So much remains unseen
despite the broad view or the absence of foliage
rolling down to the arroyo which from a certain vantage
appears swallowed up by point of view.
Drawn to it as drawn to the pointlessness of it all
after a while I couldn't tell if nostalgia was
for a place or a time or before learning to think.

The San Gabriels

She didn't allow herself to speak over the years
except in exchanges of weather, except in clichés which
betrayed only the slightest hint of more than what they were
by being so strictly put forth with no variation in tone
or raining *cats and dogs* for which there is no equivalent
thus a literal translation makes as little sense
as the care taken in the nuance of words
as the drops slip down the window or the burglar slips
in and out of the room without attracting attention
and returns to his daily round as if nothing were missing
and never mentions what's pocketed and creeping
in his brain in the shape of mist against mountains.

Not Knowing the Language

A tendency towards mannerism and widening the streets
into vacant lots dotted with waxed paper.
Not knowing the language mixes them up.
Her heart wasn't in it, her pulse said no.
Too easy to erase what from the perspective of the bird
might be *male suerte* or flying on the left hand
before the entrails were opened in the sun.
Reading the fortunes of those caught in forces
beyond the control of waiters studying to be polite
or policing the small turns of phrase
might get them to forget what the future holds.

Paraphrase

They never spoke of it.
Unless one counts the daily paraphrase.
We are told nothing more than is necessary
to keep the fiction alive
a sort of attenuated anecdote
not even dedicated to an appreciation of beauty
or the pleasures of finery tossed on a couch
or dreams beyond the purview of the most attentive.
Her restatements threw him.
She had watched herself long enough to know the out-of-focus
when she got it.
Yet they tried for simplicity
and the difference September would make.
No one expected Prague with its pink and green.
Money was out of the question.
How close to the original they could get
was more to the point.

Fire at Midnight

The sound of fire is the sound of rain skimming
the drybrush and the exchange of elements
which dizzies the effort to keep separate body and soul.
Limbs flailing about on the edge of a precipice
pictures what it's like listening to tree joints unlock
over acres of blackened terrain
and the leaps across firebreaks out of control
as the see-through scrim flutters on the grate
the sole unquiet thing.

The Blue Cold

Either it's all been said or can't be as she stands
in the blue cold. Did they say
she disappeared into the thin sheets
splitting a millimeter more or less
or the air acrid as the music teacher's breath
counting all night as high as she could go
or listening to the dialtone.
Would there ever be more than the edge of a door
where she recounted the history of the times she had seen her
which by morning was less certain than the key of c.

Griffith Park

In the blue afternoon the heat on the hand in the dust
of sage and the distance between the observer and sky
your hand and what was between us as the bush
shook out mauve as the day blew into place
we lapsed into the heat and our palms leaned into warmth
which shaped the weight of weightlessness
as the sagebrush waited for the lift of birds.
We were a bend in the wrist
as elemental beings in the theory of Paracelsus
inhabiting fire and waiting for the sun to go down.

The Bus

Long lines of limbs exposing themselves all afternoon
on a stage in relentless extrapolated motion
which given the median age no one could have known
or having twisted up torsos and bits of hair
spilled a memory of comme d'habitude, comme usually,
    [comme fin de siècle.
She didn't understand where the remark skittered toward dark
or she put her hand where it would hurt if she were what
    [she wasn't
or spoke a dialect different from the distance between them
on the bus the baby wouldn't shut up but kept on to the end
as under her breath the mother spoke to it as if it could
follow her line of reasoning *quit it* she said *just quit it.*

Driving

The film breaks into dialogue after long stretches
of the sort of silence associated with wet roads
and the sounds of tires hissing in the trees as
the wind's an artificial product of moving toward the horizon
as enclosure's only a category of mind.
And then the final exchanges about the weather first
and tentative efforts to snare the other's litany of complaints
the very act of driving was designed to eliminate any sense of.

Cactus

That the cactus flower is a tongue
is a projection no doubt of one's state of paranoia
no more a penetration of the ears
than what the driver shouted from the pickup
or a lover's gesture of refusal.
Nodes of purple bruise the plant
in the smoglike vise of hours.
Then the cool respite of evening
the passing of delusion.
I would have kept obsession locked up in my mind
but was prevented by that very thing.

The Counterfeiters

Yet if we all form assumptions in the narrow beaker
of experience where are we but behind glass slipping.
Predictable as immoral acts.
Even gratuitous fingers of scissors into rear pockets
destined to show up at this moment by what has happened before.
As insomnia purchased by lies.
As cold winds bartered for.
And so, the glass is right after all
you'll never be farther than my own mind
turning over its bedsheets, never more miles away
than thoughts pilfered from novels incriminating others.

Pico Boulevard

From behind the glass they are unmitigatedly still
or passed over. Pico is another.
Driving is to driving as from one end to the other
over bridge and vale. Their eyes unnervingly swerved.
Celan says *over wine and lostness, over*
the running out of both.
I don't find you behind any eyes you open.
After the earthquake it was closed to traffic.
I look at the eyes, the sex, the eyes.
We lap at it fearful of running out,
gulps of red wine. He says
what can the translator mean by *over?*

Neutra's Window

Behind the glass barrier by moving her lips
a woman forms exhortations. Her mind is made up.
What shadows of silence under eucalyptus
where the absence of mirrors protects children
and breaks relentless cycles of words.
Fingers over lips in early portraits marks the mastery
of silent reading, a conclusion of mouth begun by all
who suck out conclusion from the ragged spill
of palm and encumbent dust. The child reads her mind.
Silently and with the stealth of figures pilfered from story
one escapes dominion.

Drowning

The way paper layered on gauze is
what thinking is like on waking.
If she could forget the dream she always had him in the
    [same place
at the same time. He appears either in the act itself
which she hadn't witnessed
her shoes wet with brine
or lost in familiar rooms.
If she could concentrate on a particular skill
as slippery as floors and clouds
and the necessity of preparations
as unsteady as paper imitating wood.

Sunset

As a stripe of light on a wall
meets a stuccoed sky
as photographers point at the fading day
or point at women crying with their heads in their hands.
Or the heady weight of the tulip bends
over the vase and Kertesz mourns the death of his wife.
The lights startle the air into shadow
where they felt as liquid as amber in the sky
hardening hearts into gold.

The Statues

Keeping in mind contradictions
and signed agreements between members of the opposite sex
and promises unmitigated by how they had moved
or changed over time from a distance
seemed a statue photographed in another country
as if several stood in the same shoes
as easily as *he said* or *she said*.
What was covered in drapery
and from the mutilations over centuries
made it difficult to tell if it was the one they thought it was
or if given carbon dating it was not in some respects a fake.
(Once I drove into a lover's neighborhood in a roundabout
fashion just to be sure.)

The Photograph

Like the lover one can't help thinking of the photograph
a minor form that haunts the skin under cover of darkness.
Flowers fly to dust when she takes it from a shelf
having forgotten who's borrowed it before.
What was obvious was the ill-fitting of color to form
the ghostly purple outside the labia of iris
as if lying for purposes of conversation
were as mannered as streetlights throwing off ochre
and circles under eyes lit from below.

Dream

Against a backdrop of rosecolored spreads and rabbits
hanging earsdown in a farmhouse you ate poulet
and spoke perfect French. When you agreed to meet
the park swelled to a miasma of green and I passed by
in dresses from a bygone era and watched with envy
as you strolled off over the bridge over the Seine
and made my phone call home having lost the will
to speak the truth, having lost my native tongue.
Pliny tells the story of a painted curtain so lifelike
the competing artist asked to have it drawn aside.

First Street

The kimono releases white birds
where perfect flying's imbedded in cloth
dyed in thread of immersion and pulled
through endless chysanthemum skies.
Abrasion unnamed. The wounding of evening
goes on beyond where we stand behind glass.
Packing her things with no thought
or a fundamental distrust of miracle
biting the thread and balling a knot
at the tail. A dot of blood pricks wisteria.

The Sierras

Is this the middle of nowhere or a translation into thin air
as altitudes enraptured with rift.
Sierras folded over as molten sheets she puts away.
What they collapse into frayed as the bindings
betrayed by time. How many ages to make them
how sharp the intake of breath at altitudes greater than
the irregular outline of a saw bringing down pines.
Also a code word for S. Sleep and the supposed peace
it brings dream of the mute and secretive sewing
of women lifting up their hands and signing.

The Hollywood Hills

The camels of the horizon darken the park
men are meeting in. His back's against the wall.
He said, make room for the rest of us
as if sky were forever.
It was a caravan of sorts moving above the birds
squirreling their finds.
It was towards evening and the undulation
of mountains divided all in two
as if in the world to come light and dark
would be a puzzle as satisfying as
the laying down of sky on land.

No Man's Land

Between Eagle Rock and downtown drops away
before the freeway loops
and manzanita signs off reddish
in the pale light before rushhour.
Around the curve, around the bend
where no man's land carves itself
into a city frail as insistent.
Tatooed over his upperleft he can't remember how he got it
how he ended up in Elysian Park
from which the police were shipping him
home by bus in time for Christmas.

The Real

If realism is at the periphery the whole city attains
the status of a real corner where Auden exclaimed
on the dog at the intersection avoiding the gridlock
of cars. Your perfume lingers on my sleeve.
I couldn't give details enough.
If truth's impoverished by myth
by which did I get to this corner this year
through what explosions or falling papers.
If one goes in either direction long enough
it ends up as experience heady enough to get through
given the uncertain status of the real.

The Moon over LA

The moon moreover spills onto
the paving stone once under foot.
Plants it there one in front.
She is no more than any other except her shoulders forever.
Keep riding she says vacant as the face of.
Pull over and give us a kiss.
When it hangs over the interchange
she and she and she. A monument to going nowhere,
a piece of work unmade by man. O moon,
rise up and give us ourselves awash and weary—
we've seen it all and don't mind.

Not Just a Pronoun

G: Do *Not* like bird at school.
C: Is there a bird at school?
G: *Not* a bird at school.
C: Is there a big bird at school?
G: *Not* big bird at school.
C: Is there a little bird at school?
G: *Not* little bird at school.

(*lapse*)

G: *Not* real bird at school.
      Genie, the wild child of Temple City

1

It was what was seven petals, eight times two
one becomes a parody of whoever she was
hair dyed the color of dirt. Purple
impossibility of not repeating the shrug of shoulder
or evaporation into the hooting of owls.
Never mind the time counting just to pass the time,
purple tulips bagged up for possible blooms
for what will come back as shadows of a former self
mouthing the sounds of birds.

                       "Identified best by its voice, a
short nasal *car*, which may be confused with the *caw*."

2

There are none at the feeder, no brightcapped birds,
rancor in the morning and at night,
the slice of light as the door swings
and the fan cuts the air thicker than summer overall.
Leaving's as imminent as airports.
Against the sand eyes pull tight.
A sleight of hand caught in the metal door
or the bitter taste of no one's after you
just the bright bit gone,
just the flash of black wing turning blue.

3
Listening to the sounds of water over rocks
walking the side of a river with someone not unlike you
listening in the dream to the drip of water
which from your point of view evaporates into sun
which from my point of view leads to a city
overrun by airplanes she might have heard
until I can no longer find the path
by tracing threads of memory
blinded by the glare I slept in once.

4
And so, shall we say, like being under water
with the usual floating hair and and limbs
before turning to other things
this body wrinkling under us
as if one could glimpse in the mirror
what weighs them down, keeps feet on the ground.
The spongy touch gives way and breaks like dawn
over rusted-out cars beside a pool
to float our as-yet-weightless bodies on,
treading upwards and upwards for air.

        "The case was the case of escape, of living under water, of being at once impersonal and firm."

5
Almost unable to breathe in the rarified air
each brings to the occasion
bottled up as water taken for the cure.
Groping about at the mirror
wiping it off to see what's there.
Racing about as if speed etched lines
around the figure of who one was,
lying, *par exemple*, in a flowered dress
in a flowered chaise, or about the past
we dash about shapeless as water heated to prophecy—
knowing where one's going is where one's been.

6
What we say will be easy; why we say it will be difficult
as too demanding of another's turning head
with more than sympathy in mind.
I'll take even that, mindful, mindless,
gathering up the acute and the limp—
five purple tulips put in or the weather or more.
Why is diffuse and ungainly as limbs
banging into doorways and turning black and blue—
a conversation of crows sidling the lawn.

7
A room of threads overblown above us
and sticking between the teeth
chattering like daws in the wind.
They know when light is coming
and when earthquakes hold us semifrozen in the dawn.
If her face collapses in the mirror
handheld like a jittery camera and if the collapse
also of the mind she startles at her name.
The enlargement shows no scar tissue,
only bewilderment and the owl hooting a space
from which to proliferate sound.

                    "By weeping she appeared like a
single personality who, by multiplying her tears, brought
herself into the position of one who is seen twenty times in
twenty mirrors."

8
We are drinking tea and avoiding omens
foaming like yeast in the mind.
If you are shouting or not,
if I have approached with apprehension, if not.
Why the color green keeps coming to seem
the center of things isn't clear
as the sounds of birds might be from outside
or as part of the sound system
and the staccato of the director's voice.
The girl strokes the seagull matter-of-factly
having no fear for the future like green's a color.

                        Genie: "Where is tomorrow Mrs. L?
                                Where is stop spitting?"

9
No mind, no will, no listening to the wild heart.
Just so long as it doesn't rise like eels
just so long as the mother of invention
doesn't start her endless lists of demands—
one camera sliding along the sunset,
one handheld moment of dawn.
He asks if I remember my hipbones bright at the window.
He asks if I mind that he does,
I—edgy at the edges—hear a distant pounding in the ears.

10
Adjectives as the shades bottles come in
pile up as stones keep us intact.
Paint is a clue someone's been here
taken on more than passing in and out—
the abstractions of argument thrown like weight
against a slammed door or colors chosen to reflect light
pouring in at the window. *Out of it* is what is
staring towards the hills where clouds come down
like bottles on their sides:
navajo-white, oyster-pearl, blancmange.

11
The heart gathers description
like folds of molten rock.
Adjectives pool like algae,
green and broken glass in a valley.
As breaking a heart. As a green girl.
As the sketchbook opens
and the bottle towers over hope like a tower.
At the edge of the pool a glint in the eyes
as lacework's drawn aside for native oak
pencilled in broken lines through which light breaks.
The sketch pulls taut what I remember of being pulled towards.

     "In the early days before speak-
ing, she would tense up her body and take a deep breath,
then produce an extremely high-pitched sound."

12

Can it have been at such a distance before.
Or does it just keep moving like this,
centripital as the universe explains the beginning of time.
In the dream I miss the pages falling over
the bridge, the outstretched hand.
The air as thin as her skirt,
her eyelash grazing the pages she sleeps by.
No contradictions are explained or embraced
but elided music is her voice,
the thin air she's bled off into edges of ink.

13

Over the sink it's not mere rant I'm thinking
our hands disappear over time,
fade into wreckage on a hillside of rusted cars.
Close as we get to epic loss she said
all evidence of houses pulled down
these doorknobs lined up in rows, a mound of appendages
and kitchens wishing we both were to put it back
running bare feet over linoleum floors
drinking coffee gone tinny and fond.

14
One can't help the sort of certitude memory claims
though before and after is fuzzy enough the tree was
certainly willow though it sent out tendrils
over the walls, the curtains, the pillow I laid down on
and pulled my knees to my chin insisting the voice
said your name as you walked into the room as you fell
into the arms of two who knew the exact inflection.
Photos were dropping into skirts
like pieces of one torn to bits.

15
The bottlegreen dead have come again
tossing the heavy silver balls into the ring,
stitching up mouths. Over there the mother
straps on her turquoise shoes and taps awhile.
All the color of aqua milk runs out to sea.
The island carved by wind and water is blue as the eye
in a harbor she thought to tame withal.
Her salty and windblown hair, her tight face drawn tighter
into spectrums of color, a rainbow of skirts.

> "She said, 'she is myself, what am
I to do?' 'Make birds' nests with your teeth; that would be
better.'"

16
Teeth grinding the night into molecules of sand
a mouthful of wouldn't explain or there's no way
to learn the grasping at straws.
Waiting for a word drives one wild
as if others were waiting at an hallucinated corner
shattered into pinpoints of pink and green
night comes in before the glaring expanse
where clues could be hidden for years
where birds unmake themselves into darkness by sound.

17
He says you're a control freak or something like it.
As if one could will monthly blood or tears.
As if when they dry up were a matter of common sense.
It isn't only a pronoun. It isn't only the onset
of sentiment. I am walking towards you
as if it were a matter of will
through an ashy grove of olives
towards a figure native to the place
talking slowly, speaks of ease in his native tongue.

18
Exiled as the owl finds itself on a lone tree
floating sound out in a collapse of syllables
like five birds in one.
Boxed up, the cardboard head lifts its plumes—
pearls of words along a string
of floating ribbon sent out by the tongue.
What comes back's the speechless world
the miracle to stand on
as out back the warbler mimics what creaks in the wind.

                        "Some keep on copying others
around them, some have almost nothing in them of themselves inside them."

19
The world's made by birds, piece by piece chatter,
inadvertant as sky. By what memory decides.
Insistence's as foolish as stamping
a foot, she slams a door, pulls the sheets,
squeezes eyes tight. What seeing means
as two doves side by side on the telephone wire
as the jay drops in a sudden swerve behind closed lids.
The unconscious rules by night and by day
wandering along the same river twice
where the sky brightens between forks of a poplar tree.

20

What's the tone of inclination or the rancor
of wheeling through the way one thinks.
Peeling off aphorisms as labels off a bottle
I dream of wind coming up in the floorboards,
breaks into shoehorns or a cloister of song.
Where late the sweet birds sang her silence complete
even in the face of frenzy,
down one-way streets, cul-de-sacs of the mind—
the shimmer of a silver eye.

                       "Lend me a Looking-glasse.
If that her breath will mist or staine the stone,
Why then she lives."

21

To what sessions of thought gathers quiet
as breath takes its asthmatic way to faint.
I want to block you out.
The mirror held to the mouth doesn't steam up
unless hope is larger than life.
In the quiet of the vestibule I heard her breathe and sleep,
sleep and breathe while her neck gave way under the weight.
She didn't look me in the eye, her eyes were in her lap,
the fragility of skin sucking silver in.

22
The inflection not allowed, the particular tone.
A voice as acid as drinking late and early,
the exact amount measured in teaspoons,
bottle by bottle as a parade of items
seen from a height magnified as a mind.
The cupboards locked, the birdbath dry, the tulips brown.
The quality of mercy's a line of perspiration
on the lip trying to mend its ways.
The label poisons the heart,
what's sprayed on fells small birds.

23
Only one cup breaks.
The mark of sucking in, of biting one's tongue.
I pick up where I left off leading astray.
Six times three is what the child put in the round peg
or throwing the ball each time in the thorns.
The rag of skin on a thumb marks nothing
but closets carried around too long.
Who put the cup on the edge of the square
of hearts in a month of Tuesdays?
Who let her out to wander around aimless as a rose?

                      "Make love in the meadow; me
not peerless. I scar my naked hip on a wild rose."

24
Reduced to *no* in the night, all's left of a string
of protests, a string of hair chewed on to split
the ends of an argument or behind the newsprint
tongue-tied and staring out a window
the spraypaint turns on itself
inside out and upside down as Sanskrit
or the garbled effort of tying on wings.
The missing mirror of eyes, the loss of her tongue.
What would retrieve the metallic taste of her skin,
what unreasoned, unreasonable cry?

25
Semi-still, the mind hedges,
fills as a balloon of air, breaks.
An about face brings one to what one wasn't
bringing out the worse in me is what she said
lost in a woods, airless as the closet
girl-sized limbs pressed against.
Again, the hedged-at answers, the waffling reply,
the *unhuh* dribbling out the corners of a mouth.
Extreme to please and after extreme to make the taker mad.

        "Unable to vocalize, Genie
would use objects and parts of her body to make noise and
help express her frenzy: a chair scratching against the floor,
her fingers scratching against a balloon."

26
The bird opens and closes its beak.
What clamps the heart?
The wren pulls a thread from a spiral of dizziness
before the faint, before the cop-out, before cartoons come on.
The hum of a radio from the window
even though no one is home behind the fuchias.
She made no noise but turned on herself
biting, pinching, sobless,
scratches her finger on the pink balloon.

27
She keeps cropping up eager to please and horrid.
Crows loom over the desert floor
trying out for dark clouds let loose over the mountains
and blowing here as the slightest of rain.
Watch me, she says, pinching the arm of the girl with flat hair
who warbles and shifts,
her arms flapping to make the rain come,
her eyelids dark as the darkest of wings,
watch her come, she says, watch her go.

Other Minds

Imagine another mind as the lonely magazine
a year old and in the same place you left it
never thinking to return to the same place
and being without anything to read in the night
you can't sleep again you go through the same stories
gothic in intent and a bit thin you thought
the first time round getting in at the edges—
a scorch on damp paper. Or the pages
stuck together and instead of trying patiently
to pry them apart so the page ending
"he wondered if the same image wouldn't"
wouldn't end abruptly but would carry on
like love and polite as Henry James
was rumored to be and whose phrase it was.

"wings of the dove"

The mind of another balks at my saying how was it,
but how was it and who agrees about the divertimento and
who could hear with all that rain? Yet the retreat
to points of view as in you have yours and I have mine
unmindful of import and rank, a retreat
like running for cover from the rain.
What link between eyes and brain, what evidence for
what was so? Shall we ask everyone who heard
the oboe and what if they don't know the name of the oboe
and what if the man playing has the eyes of the one
on lithium who played his guitar like the mattress
he slept on in Oakland as unmade up as his mind.

"divertimento"

The mind of another wants nothing you can see
nothing you can put your hands on though Maillol says
what in hell would I do with a model when I want
to check something I go to my wife and lift her chemise.
Uccelli the same in Italian he tells me getting thinner
getting a younger version of his wife.
Seeing what another wants only when absence creates a stir,
only when the lift-off flutter betrays where the bird was
the branch a branch of absence and when
the artist rushes in to pull the curtains aside
screaming in polyglot it's missing what
have you done with it it's missing.

                                                              "absence"

When refusal makes one's mind up and sits there
waiting its pair of hunched shoulders at the gate or door
or corner of a street busy with the traffic it is busy with.
And so Eveline didn't go to South America with the man
who either did or didn't love her, either did or didn't have
a home waiting for her and either did or didn't drown.
The same story rotates around the willow tree
I sat under and knew that refusal keeps Dublin as it is.
The day kept up appearances and even weather
and the face that was wet was a mirror of the tree
named after a dinnerware set etched with a blue bridge.

                                                "the Dubliners"

The tea-colored rub of the underside
of a magnolia leaf fallen to the sidewalk winding up
a waxy splash of months before and months to come.
Tobacco-stained as fingers by the sea and matte
as a color reflecting no light as the same sea
dulled by cloud and storm. Underneath's another season.
As if with a single stick poking about for debris
an entire ocean could be fathomed by a bit of seaweed
clinging to the stick or the gesture of reaching down.

                    "stranger than fiction"

Indefatigible strangers minding the store
staring at cartons and twisting their hair
dyed the color her mother thought best
with violets and forget-me-nots she said
you wouldn't recognize my brother he's shaved
and the color of her woodbark hair peels
against the green of the velvet fields
bedecked and bejeweled as her tulle train catches
on the root of a tree and the fog comes down
the color of onions and milk driving home.

"the store"

So many spruces, two pines, how he sees
an unplanted form in the dark.
The rhythm of gray November as undifferentiated
as days of drift pulled in by a border of conifers
hedging against the cold lest it go on like cowboys
forever into the endlessly graying sky.
Vaguely unwell I see nothing in a blur of branch,
nothing that hasn't born plums for three years
and when I pick out the repeated match
of color to the long border of sloping yellow
in a distant tree, it's the one has to come down,
only the yellow form of its disease fitting it in.

"the garden"

Yours glazes over with red berries
as suddenly I see your aunt's casket
floating over black stars like an unwinding scarf,
the giddy mood of the especially somber
unfolding before me as the berries come into fruit,
as the apples scent each stone in the road
as the moths take their souls away for another season.
Only one lingering the lamp unwilling to let go
bumps the shade, the book, the shade
and settles underneath something somewhere.
A mix of moods, yours, in the somber gaiety
of how you approach with unearthly hesitation
before you go off and settle somewhere
further away than where you live.

         "end of summer"

My mind at cross-purposes, asking
what collapse might be if it weren't utter collapse.
Poppies in a season of rain
heads of petals spattering the ground,
stalky jewelweed bent double across the path
the primroses are flattened on.
Yield rather. As in *the tree always yields good fruit.*
The scent of apples on every August wind
at the edge of the stone at right angles with the path.
As in Austen's *the door yielded to her hand*
as if a single sentence could open the world up
to a view of figures and dance.

                                             "pride and prejudice"

The question of why another lifts your spirits so
and why the intake of breath
and why the tilt towards clarinets
sounded by singing into them as the air
is suddenly pierced by the needles of fir trees
falling all around, the space behind the conifers
opening up and the sky filling with stars.
She said in a sing-song, *beauty.*
She said, *the lilt of her voice.*
She said strange sounds behind the regular sounds
you have to tilt your head to hear
or the regular sounds as the sounds of birds
you come to hear them and not hear them
throughout the whole of the day even the rattling
of the tin around the telephone pole calling and calling
which two or three days later arrives and then
the silence as the flight of heavy birds.

"mythic birds"

He says his keeps slipping into hers
and you know it's no good there's a therapy name for it
I've forgot but when you hear the song
about *no tomorrows* you know that he's got it
and knows what it's like that's why I play it over
and over until I can hear it in my sleep but then
I wanted it to go away and it wouldn't and that's when
I stopped sleeping and figured it all out
like you've got to stay away from women who seem
most like you who seem to understand what's forming
under your tongue and when they touch you you can't get
the words out and you've got to keep regular hours
and set the alarm at the same time and you've got to
keep away from thinking like there's no tomorrow.

"no tomorrow"

The mindless one hovers harvest moons
over the Bonaventure and takes its pills for its supper.
Mannequins of playfulness, platitudes of manifold
attitudes it takes to get across town at this hour
and who can figure the traffic patterns and I'm sorry
I took those you had set aside for your own use
and I'm sorry I didn't let you win but was in a hurry
to get to the elevator and from this vantage
the city lays out its lights on the building
from the top of which we could get over
the queasy feeling of stomachs turned to neon pulsing
lines of traffic exposed too long to the light.

"night and day"

The gesture of an off-hand sort flicked a mind
in my direction only by the ends of the fingers
which opened a door on hinges
going one way but only by chance.
I wouldn't have chosen but given the ways of things
and the particular direction in which you stand
I let you in on a little secret.
I've said it three times to test it
to practice flyfisherman-like the hook
of fingers catching a snag of her hair.
The tree was just in the way behind the rock
on which I stood to make a cast
and the line caught and tangled as I got
a taste of what it turned out later I was after.

                        "happenstance"

The question crosses into a lane of
traffic skids on the gravel of what was left over from
another affair and how she expects betrayal
at the drop of a hat and won't let loose of it,
won't stay on the straight and narrow but
drives on without a thought for the wreckage
she thinks has been done her though
the tire marks a clear sign of the out-of-control
she's taken as a route through what seems to her
printed on the map. The way is unclear.
The accident isn't planned. The tree is not
a sign of the raw stubbornness of the world.

         "accidents will happen"

Unless you are a god, he says, the mind
is entirely unlike the body. Why then do my joints ache
when I think of it, why do I think of flight.
The heron at the side of the island
is a white question mark. The blue one insists,
lifting its head to stare. What I forgot to say
lodges in my legs and the weight drags
on the floor. Shore birds go in and out
as if they couldn't bear wet feet
as if water were an element unavoidable
and necessary, a mental equivalent of wing.

                                             "the great blue"

Getting at it,
scissors cutting away the frippery,
the affectations of lace.
And what's yours, my love,
dear as the eyes won't ever meet mine?
Or selvage discarded and then only then found to be
the very thing.
Patterns running through the cloth
or the crack at the center of the bowl.
A way in might be the eyes
but remember the one on lithium,
the depths all shallowed,
the marble glints in muddy disarray
like a bit fished from the edge of a pond
and the mind with that clear fissure running through
just the cold wash hanging on the line, cold wind blowing through.

"the golden bowl"

Memory's tenacious, so where is he
when part of what you think or mean to say
depends on what's said in return.
Why is it this that returns,
not so much wrist or skin
but the fretful turning about of one's own mind
to find part of it missing
walked off down the street with a perfect stranger
who said what they always say
until the rhythm of walking seems a rhythm
you'll always hear like waves if you lived by the sea.
But when you stop you hear only one set of footfalls
stopped beneath your feet and a racing about somewhere
and a heart beating a reply.

                               "the missing body"

Caught in gyrations of weather,
the other's equivalent to cloud.
It prints the distance with a milky smudge,
comes down as far as the garden, sits on
the steps. What seems tangible
becomes a damp scrim of brow,
a slight sign on your skin.
A curtain of rain won't fall.
Before you can put a finger on what seems
certain as petals it's moved away.
No will in this. No defiance or mock.
The plain properties of water, arabesque.

                              "equivalents"

New American Poetry Series (NAP)

1. *Fair Realism*, Barbara Guest
[now Sun & Moon Classics: 41]
2. *Some Observations of a Stranger at Zuni in the Latter Part of the Century*, Clarence Major
3. *A World*, Dennis Phillips
4. *A Shelf in Woop's Clothing*, Mac Wellman
5. *Sound As Thought*, Clark Coolidge
6. *By Ear*, Gloria Frym
7. *Necromance*, Rae Armantrout
8. *Loop*, John Taggart
[now Sun & Moon Classics: 150]
9. *Our Nuclear Heritage*, James Sherry
10. *Arena*, Dennis Phillips
11. *I Don't Have Any Paper So Shut Up*, Bruce Andrews
12. *An American Voyage*, Joe Ross
13. *Into Distances*, Aaron Shurin
14. *Sunday's Ending Too Soon*, Charley George
15. *Letters of the Law*, Tom Mandel
16. *To Give It Up*, Pam Rehm
[WINNER NATIONAL POETRY SERIES 1995]
17. *Asia & Haiti*, Will Alexander
18. *Sentences*, Charles O. Hartman and Hugh Kenner
19. *How To Do Things with Words*, Joan Retallack
20. *Made to Seem*, Rae Armantrout
21. *State of Mind*, Martha Ronk
22. *Elemenopy*, Michael Coffey
23. *Credence*, Dennis Phillips
24. *Noon*, Cole Swensen
[WINNER NEW AMERICAN POETRY SERIES COMPETITION 1995]
25. *A Door*, Aaron Shurin
26. *Lotion Bullwhip Giraffe*, Tan Lin
28. *Dura*, Myung Mi Kim
29. *The Disparities*, Rodrigo Toscano
30. *Designated Heartbeat*, Bruce Andrews

31. *Polyverse*, Lee Ann Brown
[WINNER NEW AMERICAN POETRY SERIES COMPETITION 1995]
32. *Response*, Juliana Spahr
[WINNER NATIONAL POETRY SERIES 1995]

For a complete list of our poetry publications
write us at Sun & Moon Press
6026 Wilshire Boulevard
Los Angeles, California 90036